Fly Away Home

By Eve Bunting

Illustrated by Ronald Himler

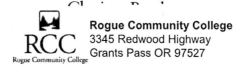

Rogue Community College
3345 Redwood Highway
Grants Pass OR 97527

RCC
Rogue Community College

Clarion Books
a Houghton Mifflin Company imprint
215 Park Avenue South, New York, NY 10003
Text copyright © 1991 by Eve Bunting
Illustrations copyright © 1991 by Ron Himler, Inc.

The text type is 14-point Sabon.
The illustrations for this book were executed in watercolor.

Printed in China

Library of Congress Cataloging-in-Publication Data
Bunting, Eve, 1928–
Fly away home / Eve Bunting ; illustrated by Ronald Himler.
p.   cm.
Summary: A homeless boy who lives in a airport with his father, moving from
terminal to terminal and trying not to be noticed, is given hope when he
sees a trapped bird find its freedom.
ISBN 0-395-55962-6   PA ISBN 0-395-66415-2
[1. Homeless persons—Fiction. 2. Airports—Fiction. 3. Birds—Fiction.]
I. Himler, Ronald, ill. II. Title.
PZ7.B91527F1 1991
[E]—dc20   90-42353
CIP
AC

SCP   48   47
4500577282

To Jim Giblin,
my friend and editor

—E.B.

My dad and I live in an airport. That's because we don't have a home and the airport is better than the streets. We are careful not to get caught.

Mr. Slocum and Mr. Vail were caught last night.

"Ten green bottles, hanging on the wall," they sang. They were as loud as two moose bellowing.

Dad says they broke the first rule of living here. Don't get noticed.

Dad and I try not to get noticed. We stay among the crowds. We change airlines.

"Delta, TWA, Northwest, we love them all," Dad says. He and I wear blue jeans and blue T-shirts and blue jackets. We each have a blue zippered bag with a change of blue clothes. Not to be noticed is to look like nobody at all.

Once we saw a woman pushing a metal cart full of stuff. She wore a long, dirty coat and she lay down across a row of seats in front of Continental Gate 6. The cart, the dirty coat, the lying down were all noticeable. Security moved her out real fast.

Dad and I sleep sitting up. We use different airport areas.

"Where are we tonight?" I ask.

Dad checks his notebook. "Alaska Air," he says. "Over in the other terminal."

That's OK. We like to walk.

We know some of the airport regulars by name and by sight. There's Idaho Joe and Annie Frannie and Mars Man. But we don't sit together.

"Sitting together will get you noticed faster than anything," Dad says.

Everything in the airport is on the move—passengers, pilots, flight attendants, cleaners with their brooms. Jets roar in, close to the windows.

Other jets roar out. Luggage bounces down chutes, esca-
lators glide up and down, disappearing under floors. Every-
one's going somewhere except Dad and me. We stay.

Once a little brown bird got into the main terminal and couldn't get out. It fluttered in the high, hollow spaces. It threw itself at the glass, fell panting on the floor, flew to a tall, metal girder, and perched there, exhausted.

"Don't stop trying," I told it silently. "Don't! You can get out!"

For days the bird flew around, dragging one wing. And then it found the instant when a sliding door was open and slipped through. I watched it rise. Its wing seemed OK.

"Fly, bird," I whispered. "Fly away home!"

Though I couldn't hear it, I knew it was singing. Nothing made me as happy as that bird.

The airport's busy and noisy even at night. Dad and I sleep anyway. When it gets quiet, between two and four A.M., we wake up.

"Dead time," Dad says. "Almost no flights coming in or going out."

At dead time there aren't many people around, so we're extra careful.

In the mornings Dad and I wash up in one of the bathrooms, and he shaves. The bathrooms are crowded, no matter how early. And that's the way we like it.

Strangers talk to strangers.

"Where did you get in from?"

"Three hours our flight was delayed. Man! Am I bushed!"

Dad and I, we don't talk to anyone.

We buy doughnuts and milk for breakfast at one of the
cafeterias, standing in line with our red trays. Sometimes
Dad gets me a carton of juice.

On the weekends Dad takes the bus to work. He's a jani-
tor in an office in the city. The bus fare's a dollar each way.

On those days Mrs. Medina looks out for me. The Medinas live in the airport, too—Grandma, Mrs. Medina, and Denny, who's my friend.

He and I collect rented luggage carts that people have left outside and return them for fifty cents each. If the crowds are big and safe, we offer to carry bags.

"Get this one for you, lady? It looks heavy."

Or, "Can I call you a cab?" Denny's real good at calling cabs. That's because he's seven already.

Sometimes passengers don't tip. Then Denny whispers, "Stingy!" But he doesn't whisper too loud. The Medinas understand that it's dangerous to be noticed.

When Dad comes home from work, he buys hamburgers for us and the Medinas. That's to pay them for watching out for me. If Denny and I've had a good day, we treat for pie. But I've stopped doing that. I save my money in my shoe.

"Will we ever have our own apartment again?" I ask Dad. I'd like it to be the way it was, before Mom died.

"Maybe we will," he says. "If I can find more work. If we can save some money." He rubs my head. "It's nice right here, though, isn't it, Andrew? It's warm. It's safe. And the price is right."

But I know he's trying all the time to find us a place. He takes newspapers from the trash baskets and makes pencil circles around letters and numbers. Then he goes to the phones. When he comes back he looks sad. Sad and angry. I know he's been calling about an apartment. I know the rents are too high for us.

"I'm saving money, too," I tell him, and I lift one foot and point to my shoe.

Dad smiles. "Atta boy!"

"If we get a place, you and your dad can come live with us," Denny says.

"And if *we* get a place, you and your mom and your grandma can come live with *us*," I say.

"Yeah!"

We shake on it. That's going to be so great!

After next summer, Dad says, I have to start school.

"How?" I ask.

"I don't know. But it's important. We'll work it out."

Denny's mom says he can wait for a while. But Dad says I can't wait.

Sometimes I watch people meeting people.

"We missed you."

"It's so good to be home."

Sometimes I get mad, and I want to run at them and push them and shout, "Why do *you* have homes when we don't? What makes *you* so special?" That would get us noticed, all right.

Sometimes I just want to cry. I think Dad and I will be here forever.

Then I remember the bird. It took a while, but a door opened. And when the bird left, when it flew free, I know it was singing.